Snow White

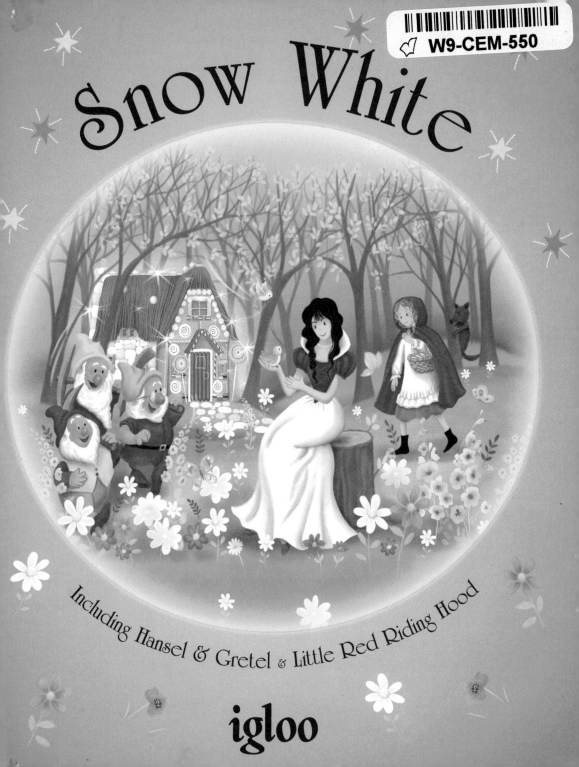

Including Hansel & Gretel & Little Red Riding Hood

igloo

Snow White

ne winter's day, a Queen sat at a window, sewing. Suddenly, she pricked her finger and a drop of blood fell onto the snow below. She liked the bright red of the blood against the whiteness of the snow. She hoped that one day she would give birth to a child with lovely, snow-white skin and bright, blood-red lips.

The very next year, the Queen gave birth to a baby daughter. The baby had the whitest of skin and the reddest of lips. The Queen called her child Snow White and she loved her daughter dearly. Sadly, the Queen died the very same year.

After some time, Snow White's father, the King, married again. His new Queen was very beautiful but she was also vain and proud. She owned a special mirror, and every morning she asked the mirror the same question.

"Mirror, mirror, on the wall, who is the fairest of them all?"

"You are, O Queen," the mirror would also reply.

And every morning the Queen would smile to herself, for she knew that the mirror always told the truth.

As the years passed, Snow White was slowly turning into a beautiful young woman. One morning, the Queen awoke and asked the mirror her usual question.

"Mirror, mirror, on the wall, who is the fairest of them all?"

But this time, the mirror replied:

"You, O Queen, are fair, it's true, but Snow White is now fairer than you."

The Queen turned green with envy. No one was allowed to be more beautiful than her. Even though Snow White was dearly loved by the King, the twisted, jealous Queen decided to have her killed as soon as possible. She summoned the royal huntsman and told him to take Snow White into the forest and kill her. She told him to cut out Snow White's heart and bring it to her, to prove that she was dead.

The huntsman took Snow White into the forest, but, as he was about to kill her, looked at her frightened face. He felt so sorry for her, he told her to run away and hide in the forest. Then he killed a wild boar and cut out its heart so he could pretend that it was Snow White's heart.

Snow White ran further and further into the forest until she noticed a small cottage, half hidden by the trees. She went up to the cottage and knocked on the door. There was no reply. She opened the door and went in.

In front of her was a little table with seven little cups and plates on it. The cottage belonged to seven dwarfs who worked all day in a silver mine. Snow White was very hungry and thirsty, so she took a little bit of food from each plate, and a little bit of water from each cup. After she'd eaten, she felt very tired. She went upstairs and found a room with seven beds in it. She lay down on one of the beds and fell fast asleep.

When the seven dwarfs returned home and found Snow White sleeping in one of their beds, they woke her and asked her what she was doing there. Snow White burst into tears and told them her terrible story. The seven dwarfs felt so sorry for her, they invited her to stay with them. "But I can't pay you anything for my food and bed," Snow White cried. The dwarfs told her, that as long as she cooked and kept the cottage clean for them, she was welcome to stay as long as she liked. "Thank you so much." said Snow White, happily.

Back at the castle, the wicked Queen took what she thought was Snow White's heart and had great pleasure feeding it to the dogs. The next morning, she stood in front of her mirror.
"Mirror, mirror, on the wall, who is the fairest of them all?"
"You, O Queen, are fair, it's true, but Snow White is still fairer than you," the mirror replied.
The Queen screamed in anger. She knew that the mirror never lied, so Snow White must still be alive. She found out where Snow White was living and decided to play a horrible trick on her. The Queen dis-guised herself as a peddler selling little trinkets, pieces of lace and pretty brooches, and went to the dwarfs' cottage and knocked on the door.

"Hello, my dear," croaked the Queen, pretending to be the peddler. "I've got some lovely little things here you may care to see."
"Oh, isn't it lovely!" Snow White exclaimed, as the Queen held up a pretty bow.

The Queen convinced Snow White that she needed a new length of braid for her bodice but, when she helped Snow White put it on, she pulled it so tightly that all the breath went out of Snow White's body. The Queen left her, believing she was dead.

When the seven dwarfs arrived home from work that evening, they were shocked to find Snow White lying on the floor. She didn't seem to be breathing. When they saw how tightly her bodice was tied, they quickly cut it loose. The dwarfs were relieved and delighted when she started to breathe again. They made her promise them that she'd never accept anything from a stranger in future.

Meanwhile, the Queen rushed back to the palace, ripped off her disguise and stood in front of her mirror.

"Mirror, mirror, on the wall, who is the fairest of them all?" she asked. "You, O Queen, are fair, it's true, but Snow White is still fairer than you," the mirror replied. The Queen was speechless with rage when she realised that Snow White was still alive.
"I'll think of another way to trick her," she thought.

The Queen picked an apple that had one red side and one yellow side. She then injected a deadly poison into the red side and disguised herself this time as an old peasant woman. She went to the dwarfs' cottage and knocked on the door again. Snow White was a little wary at first, but the old peasant woman was so nice and friendly, she quickly relaxed and they were soon chatting away.

After they had been talking for some time, the disguised Queen offered Snow White the poisoned apple.
"That's very kind of you," said Snow White. "But I'm not supposed to take anything from strangers."

"Don't worry. There's nothing wrong with this apple," said the Queen. "And to prove it to you, I'll take a bite out of it first."
With a great crunch, the Queen took a large bite out of the yellow side of the apple.

Then she offered the poisoned, red side to Snow White.
"I suppose it's all right, and it does look delicious," said Snow White.
As soon as she had taken a bite out of the apple, the poor girl fell dead at the Queen's feet. The Queen rushed back to the palace and ripped off her disguise. "Mirror, mirror, on the wall, who is the fairest of them all?" she asked the mirror. "You are, O Queen," it replied. The Queen shrieked with joy. She had succeeded. Snow White was well and truly dead.

When the dwarfs arrived home that evening, they could not wake Snow White. They stayed with her all night, hoping that she might wake up, but in the morning they realized that she must be dead. Snow White remained beautiful, even in death.

Years passed, and news of Snow White's beauty had spread far and wide. One day, a Prince decided to see the beautiful girl for himself. Her beauty took his breath away and he fell in love with her instantly. Tenderly, the Prince lifted Snow White's head to kiss her. But as he did so, the tiny piece of apple that had poisoned her, fell from her lips. Gradually, she began to stir. "What has happened?" she asked drowsily. The seven dwarfs jumped up and down with joy that she was alive.

When Snow White's father, the King, heard of the terrible things the Queen had done to his daughter, he banished her from his land forever. Before long, Snow White and her Prince were married. But she never forgot the kindness the seven dwarfs had shown her for the rest of her life.

Hansel and Gretel

here was once a woodcutter and his wife who lived in a tiny cottage, on the edge of a magnificent forest, with their two children. They had a boy called Hansel and a girl called Gretel. It was a hard life and there never seemed to be enough food.

The woodcutter's wife turned to her husband one night. "There's not enough bread for us all tomorrow," she said. "It would be best for everyone if you took the children into the forest and left them there."
"But they'll starve to death!" exclaimed the woodcutter.
"It's either them or us," replied his heartless wife. The woodcutter tried to make his wife change her mind, but after much argument, he reluctantly agreed to leave his children in the forest the following day.

Meanwhile, Hansel had overheard his mother and father arguing. When he heard of their terrible plan, he crept outside, picked up some white pebbles and put them in his pocket. Early the next morning, the woodcutter told his children that they must help carry the wood that he was going to chop down that day. As they walked deeper into the forest, Hansel began to drop behind him the pebbles he had collected.
"What are you doing?" Gretel asked him.
"Sshh! You'll find out," replied her brother.

After walking for many hours, the woodcutter told his children to rest while he started to cut down the trees. The children were tired after walking so far and slowly drifted off to sleep on the forest floor. When they awoke, it was night, and very dark. They realized that their father had left them in the forest, completely alone.

"I'm frightened," said Gretel, clutching her brother's arm.
"Don't worry," said Hansel. "Do you remember those white pebbles I
dropped on the way here? If we follow them, they'll lead us home."
Sure enough, the children followed the trail of white pebbles that
gleamed in the dark, and they arrived home just as the sun had started to
lighten the sky.

Early the next morning, Hansel and Gretel's mother gave them each a
chunk of bread and told them that they must help their father in the
forest again. This time, clever Hansel tore off little bits of the bread and
dropped them behind him as they walked along the path.
Once again, the woodcutter urged his children to rest as he began his
work. They were so tired, they soon fell into a long sleep.

When the children woke up, they realized that their father had left them again. "What are we going to do?" asked Gretel, nervously.

"We'll just follow the bits of bread," Hansel replied, But as hard as they looked, the children couldn't find any pieces of bread, anywhere! "Oh no!" cried Hansel. "The birds must have eaten it all."

That night, it was so cold the children walked around the forest, trying to keep warm. As the sun started to come up, they saw a white bird in the sky that seemed to be beckoning to them. Having no other plan, they followed the bird, which led them to a little cottage. They were amazed to see that the cottage walls were made entirely out of bread, the roof was iced ginger cake and the windows were made of sparkling sugar. Hansel and Gretel were so hungry they immediately began to tear bits of bread off the walls and ravenously started to eat it.

Just then, a little voice rang out:
"Nibble, nibble, little mouse,
Who's that nibbling at my house?"
Then the door opened and a little old lady came out. Hansel and Gretel thought they might be punished for eating bits of her house but the old lady simply smiled and said, "My goodness! You children must be hungry. Come inside and I'll make you breakfast."
The old lady made Hansel and Gretel a delicious breakfast. "Aren't we lucky to have found this kind lady?" said Gretel as she got into bed.

But the kind old lady was not a kind old lady at all. She was, in fact, a horrible, nasty witch who enjoyed roasting children in her oven so that she could eat them!

The next morning, she locked Hansel in a large cage and told Gretel to cook food for her brother. "He needs fattening up before he's ready for my oven," she hissed.

Each day, the witch told Hansel to stick a finger through the bars so she could feel how fat he was getting. But Hansel was clever and, instead of poking out his finger, he stuck a little bone out, to make the witch think he wasn't putting on any weight at all!

After a month, the witch was getting impatient and decided to eat Hansel straight away. She ordered Gretel to make a fire in the oven, then told her to get into it to make sure it was hot enough. Poor Gretel knew the witch would close the door behind her and roast her as well.

"I'm not very good at climbing into things. Could you show me how, please?" Gretel asked the witch. "Oh, all right," said the witch, who opened the door and crawled inside the oven to show exactly how it should be done. But, when the witch was halfway in, Gretel pushed her all the way with a great shove, and slammed the door shut behind her. And that was the end of a very horrible witch.

Gretel released her brother from the cage and they searched the cottage for anything that might be useful. They were amazed to find that the cottage was crammed full of gold coins and precious jewels. They gathered it all up and left.

After wandering for a long time, they saw smoke rising from a chimney in the distance. They were overjoyed to see that it was their cottage.

When their father saw his children were alive and well, he dropped his axe and hugged them close to him. When he saw the treasure that they had brought with them, he couldn't believe his eyes, they were rich!

Although their cruel mother had died while they were lost in the forest, the children and their father lived happily together for the rest of their days.

Little Red Riding Hood

 nce upon a time there was a nice little girl who lived with her mother in a nice little cottage at the edge of a deep, dark forest. The girl was known as Little Red Riding Hood because she always wore a beautiful red cape with a hood.

One day, her mother called to her from the kitchen. "Little Red Riding Hood, Granny is not feeling very well. Will you take her some goodies I've packed for her?"
"Of course I will," said Little Red Riding Hood, who loved her Granny very much.

Granny's cottage lay on the other side of the forest. "Now, remember," said Little Red Riding Hood's mother, "keep to the path and don't talk to any strangers."
"I won't," replied Little Red Riding Hood and, picking up the basket, she skipped merrily out the door. It was a lovely day and Little Red Riding Hood sang a merry tune to herself as she made her way along the path.

A little while later, when she was in the deepest, darkest part of the forest, she saw some pretty flowers growing in a small clearing just off the path. "I'm sure Mother wouldn't mind if I went off the path for a minute to pick some flowers. Granny would love them," she thought. She had a quick look around, didn't see anyone, so ran to the little clearing, where she started to pick the flowers.

But, hiding behind a tree, was a not-very-nice wolf, who was hungry and looking for his dinner. In one swift movement, he was at Little Red Riding Hood's side.

"Hello, my dear," he said, in his most charming voice. "What a beautiful day! I see you're picking flowers. May I help you?"

Little Red Riding Hood was startled to see the wolf at first, but he seemed so friendly and had such a lovely deep voice, her fears faded away. "I'm picking them for my Granny. She's not very well. I'm taking her this basket of food."

"What a lovely thing to do!" exclaimed the wolf, thinking that if he was clever, he might be able to eat the girl, her Granny and the basket of food for his dinner.

"I've got an idea," said the wolf. "Why don't I run ahead and give the basket to your Granny, while you finish picking your pretty flowers. Then we can all meet at her house. Hmm?"

"That's a very good idea," said Little Red Hiding Hood. "She lives a little further up the path in the first cottage."

"That's settled, then," said the wolf, taking the basket from her. "By the way, what's your name?"

"Little Red Riding Hood," she answered.

"Charmed to meet you, my dear," said the wolf, with a big, wide grin. "See you soon."

And he set off down the path towards Granny's cottage, licking his lips.

When he arrived at Granny's cottage, he knocked on the door.

"Who's there?" asked Granny, tucked up in bed.

"It's me, Granny," said the wolf, "Little Red Riding Hood."

"Come in, dear," said Granny. "I'm in bed."

The wolf opened the door and ran upstairs, into Granny's bedroom.

"You're not Little Red Riding Hood!" exclaimed Granny.

"You're absolutely right!" said the wolf, and before she had a chance to say anything else, he leapt over to her bedside, opened his mouth as wide as he could, and gobbled Granny right up. He put on Granny's shawl, nightcap and glasses as fast as he could, and dived into the bed.

"What a clever wolf I am," he chuckled to himself.

A short time later, Little Red Riding Hood arrived at Granny's cottage and knocked on the door.

"Who's there?" asked the wolf in his best Granny voice.

"It's me, Granny. Little Red Riding Hood," said Little Red Riding Hood.

"Let yourself in, dear," said the wolf.

Little Red Riding Hood opened the door and went into Granny's bedroom.